For Katie, Ben, and George
—D.L.

Clarion Books
3 Park Avenue
New York, New York 10016

First published in the U.K. in 2018 by Frances Lincoln Children's Books,
an imprint of the Quarto Group.
The Old Brewery, 6 Blundell Street, London N7 9BH, United Kingdom.
Published in the U.S. in 2019.

Clarion Books is an imprint of Houghton Mifflin Harcourt Publishing Company.

hmhco.com

The illustrations in this book were done in mixed media.
The text was set in Granjon LT.

Library of Congress Cataloging-in-Publication Data is available.
ISBN 978-1-328-59589-8

Manufactured in China
10 9 8 7 6 5 4 3 2 1
4500741708

The Bear, the Piano, the Dog, and the Fiddle

BY David Litchfield

CLARION BOOKS
Houghton Mifflin Harcourt
Boston New York

the Heroic
HECTOR

Hector and Hugo were best friends. Hector was a fiddle player, and Hugo was one of his biggest fans.

Over the years, they'd had good times, bad times, and even some crazy times.

But now times weren't so great.

"What are we going to do, Hugo?" Hector said as they walked home. "My act is yesterday's news. Who'd want to listen to an old fiddler like me, when they can watch a world-famous piano-playing bear?"

Hugo woofed to say that *he* would, but Hector just sighed.

"I'm too old for this game, boy," he said. "I guess I'll never get to play in a big concert hall, like I dreamed."

And with that, Hector packed away his fiddle forever.

Now that Hector didn't go out to play music,
he spent most of his time watching TV,

listening to audiobooks,

sleeping,

sleeping,

and sleeping some more.

Hector and Hugo's neighborhood was noisy, so Hector kept the windows shut when he slept. But one night, he forgot.

In the early hours of the morning, a strange noise woke him up.

Hector crept
out of bed,

tiptoed down
the hallway,

and pushed open
the door to the roof.

Hugo was playing Hector's fiddle,
and the music Hugo was making was
toe-tappingly,
finger-clickingly,
whistle-blowingly
AWESOME!

Hector's tummy hurt a bit
when he saw everyone in the
neighborhood nodding along,
but then he saw something else . . .

how much his friend *loved* to play.

The next morning, Hector taught Hugo all the tricks of the trade he'd learned over the years.

Before long, a crowd had gathered.

News of the incredible fiddle-playing dog spread,
and one day, a very famous bear came to watch.

Bear told Hugo that he was starting a band of musical animals. He invited him to come on tour and play his fiddle for hundreds of thousands of people.

As Hugo looked up at Hector, his tail wagging, Hector's tummy started to hurt again. He was jealous.

"I guess you should go," he said, trying to smile. "It's the opportunity of a lifetime."

Hugo's tail wagged even more as he packed to go away with Bear's Big Band, making sure the fiddle was safely stowed.

But Hector began to have second thoughts.
"Don't go and join that silly group, Hugo," he said. "We don't need them."

Hugo put his head on Hector's knee,
but Hector pushed him away.

"Fine," said Hector. "I'm sure you'll be back with your tail between your legs. You're not even that good!"

Hugo picked up his suitcase and left.
Suddenly, Hector felt awful. "*Wait*, Hugo," he cried.
"I'm sor—"

BEAR'S BIG BAND BUS
BBB

But it was too late.

With Bear's Big Band, Hugo
toured the world, playing spectacular
shows to sold-out crowds of adoring fans.

Hugo was the star of the show,

with Bear on the piano, “Big G” on drums,

and Clint “the Wolfman” Jones grooving on the double bass.

Millions of people watched them all over the world
on their televisions and computer screens . . .

millions of people, including Hector.
As he watched, he missed making music.
He missed playing his fiddle.

But most of all, he missed his friend.

One day, Hector saw some posters announcing that Bear's band was playing at the big concert hall in his city.

Hector wanted to go, but then he
remembered the horrible thing he had said.

What if Hugo didn't want him there?

Hector bought a ticket anyway and found a spot up front, right by the stage. He noticed that Hugo had a new fiddle and wondered what had happened to his old one. But then the band started playing.

Hector couldn't believe how mind-blowingly, toe-tappingly, finger-clickingly AWESOME the music was!

"Hugo!" he shouted. "It's me, Hector. You're brilliant! I'm so proud of you."

But Hugo just whispered something to Bear, who whispered something to a security guard. Then they continued to play.

A few minutes later, Hector felt two big paws grab him.

"What's going on?" he asked nervously.

The security guards picked up Hector and took him into a dark corridor.

"It's okay," Hector said, "I was going to leave anyway. *Let me go!*"

But the guards just kept walking with Hector squished between them, until suddenly they stopped.

And Hector realized where he was.

"Ladies and gentlemen," boomed a voice, "I'm pleased to announce that tonight Bear's Big Band will be joined by a *very* special guest. . ."

"Please give a warm welcome to Hector. I'm told that our star, Hugo, wouldn't be here without him."

As the crowd cheered, Hugo passed Hector his old fiddle. He'd kept it safe all this time. He woofed and wagged his tail.

And as Hector took his fiddle, he realized that though he and Hugo might have some good times, some bad times, and even some times apart, they would still always be friends.

Because good friendship,
just like good music,
lasts a lifetime.